The Three Year

Affair

By: Anny Omous

This is an engrossing story full of surprises, darkness, and betrayal. The author's humor shows through frequently ("Fuck the cops. Oh ya, you just did"), and the character of Anny will garner readers' sympathy for her uncensored humanity. The book is structurally tight, with chapters that alternate points of view between Liam and Anny and a narrative drive that will keep readers engaged.

Kirkus Reviews

Reader Reviews

So just finished it and all I have to say is when the #### is the next one ready??? Loved it! Can't wait for number two.
Vicki C.
Pembroke, Ontario

Wow! Love the book!
Kim G.
Fredericton, New Brunswick

I love this book! It's the ONLY book I took the time to read in 10 years, because I couldn't put it down!!! Can't wait for the next one!!!
Tara N.
Rutherglen, Ontario

Just read your book and it is awesome!
Serenna B.
Timmins, Ontario

So badass!!
Alexus O.
Redbridge, Ontario

Just finished your book. Very well done. It kept you wanting to keep reading to find out the next crazy thing she was gonna pull next... I look forward to the next one!

Keith P.
North Bay, Ontario

Read your book today and it left me wanting more… I'd say that's a damn good sign! Keep up the good work, you rock.
Michele C.
Burlington, Ontario

Can't wait for the next one!!!!
Patricia R.
Grand Valley, Ontario

Amazing read people… If you haven't got it yet go and get it!
Jody E.
Redbridge, Ontario

Publishing & Credit Notes

Published by Anny Omous Publishing

Anny Omous Publishing, P.O. Box 205, Katrine, Ontario, Canada, P0A 1L0

Distributed by Lulu.com

Published in this second edition 2015

Publisher's note: This book is a work of fiction. Names, characters, places and incidents
either are the product of the author's imagination or are used fictitiously, and any
resemblance to actual persons, living or dead, events, or locales is entirely coincidental.

Library and Archives Canada Cataloguing in Publication
Omous-Anny/2014
The Three Year Affair/Anny Omous
ISBN 978-0-9938933-4-6
EBook ISBN 978-0-9938933-5-3

Cover design and photography: Brian Boudreau Photography
Tattoo by: Caleb Atkinson, Dead City Studios
Formatting by: Alana Healey & Danielle Bensen
Copy Edited by: William LaRochelle

threeyearaffair@wordpress.com

Dedication

To my Muse:

*T*hank you for giving me the courage to step from the shadows into the light, the passion to lust for life again, and the strength to hold strong to my convictions. For these things know that you will always own a piece of my heart.

Intro

I could feel his breath on my neck between kisses, as my back hit the wall in the otherwise an un-occupied men's room. The intense feelings of panic and desire ran though my body all at once.

"We have to stop. They're gonna realize if we are gone too long." I said between breaths.

"No they won't. We'll be quick." He said, trying to keep my attention on the task at hand.

"Holy fuck." I whispered, as I tried and fight the urge to open his belt buckle that my fingers somehow had found. His hands travelled down my body, grabbing and pulling me into the swirling tornado of passion that had found my centre of being.

"We have to stop! Not here, not here!" I said this time with fortitude.
He leaned his head on to my neck and tried to control his breathing. His body pressed hard against mine, I felt his excitement, as he tried to gather himself. I ran my fingers up the back of his neck and through his thick dark hair, trying to catch my breath as well.

"Okay, but this is far from over!" He whispered in my ear. He leaned down and kissed me. I tried for a second one. He grinned a seductive smile and pulled away, teasing me, making me want him more. Then, after what felt like forever, he leaned in for the final kiss of the session. I went weak under his control, and in that moment I knew I was fucked.

Chapter One

Returning to the table separately was actually quite easier than I had thought. The table full of half-drunk, high school, alumni, would never suspect what we had just been up to. Thank God! How could they? We were certainly not each other's type. I had too many close friends there that could bust me in a second with one look. Not that they would, just that the details of my dirty little secret had never been discussed. Judgment and outrage would most likely ensue, considering my current long-term relationship of nine years was still in full swing, with a very different man than the one that nearly made me orgasm in the bathroom. I took a long swig of my double rum drink I so cleverly named, fuck me it's Friday, and decided I needed a second away from the crowd. So I headed for a smoke outside.

Outside in the cold air, the thoughts in my head were swimming. *What the fuck was I doing? How the fuck could I not do this! Oh my God I am insane! How did we go from Facebook friends, to Facebook fuck friends, to actual fuck friends? The twenty-five hundred kilometers of distance between us had always made me feel like there was a safety net around this whole thing. How am I gonna control this? I can't control myself with him... and in all honesty, I knew I didn't want to.* Fuck me, this was gonna be a hell of a night!

My inner monologue had started playing: *Calm down. You can handle this, relax.* The one that could always draw me out of a panic attack, just enough, to keep others from noticing, and me passing out. I could hear the door of the restaurant open. I turned to see a couple of my girlfriends coming out for a smoke. I tried to gather my thoughts, and prepare for a regular conversation.

"Hey girl, what's up?" Said Sara

"Not much man, just enjoying the night." I answer back.

"It's so funny seeing Liam." She says as she lights her smoke. "He thinks tonight is all about him. Remember when everyone used to tease him back in the day, because he was so tall and lanky, and had glasses?"

"Hey man whatever! He planned this event, so I guess it is about him a bit!" I caught myself snarling back, surprising myself in the process. "Besides, he's cool! I talk to him all the time."

"Oh ya, no doubt, buddy,' she said kind of back-pedaling. I finished the last drag of my smoke and flick it in the butt can.

"Well I'm fucking freezing. I'll see ya in there," I said, heading to the door. I could hear them responding back, but I was too inside my own head to really listen. The one thing I couldn't stand was people who talked shit about others to make themselves look better. I never could. It was right then when a flash of a moment splashed through my head. Amazingly so clear, which for me was rare. So much of my childhood was in a current and consistent state of blackout, that it was costing the federal government thousands for my two current shrinks to play around in my head. A flash, and a moment that made me panic just a little and question if fate was a sadist.

It's funny when you have little recollection of your past. My friends were always asking remember when we did this, or remember this person? Sometimes I would say yes just to avoid hearing the entire tale. Sadly, the majority of the time the answer was no. But now this: A strange and funny memory.

1984 - 30 years prior - Age 8

I remember it being a spring day. The grass was kind of wet and the wind a bit warm. I turned the corner of the school to see three classmates' laughing and pushing around an eight year old Liam. I remember the feeling of my face burning from it turning red in anger. I ran towards the crowd yelling, before slapping one of them really hard across the face. The boy whose face I hit turned to me. His face was turning red from the impact, as he tried to hold in the tears of humiliation and shock in his eyes. I grabbed Liam's hand and started to walk away with him. Liam was bewildered and quiet. As I did, I could hear the wounded one call out.

"OOOOWWWW, look they're holding hands. They must be married," he said. I stopped, spun on my heel, and screamed.

"You bet! Your right! Bug him again and I'll kick you in the nuts, asshole." Then I turned and kissed Liam on the cheek in front of everyone. We walked away holding hands.

It's bizarre how such a stupid memory could suddenly shake up one's whole outlook on life? Was this some fucking twisted sign that now, fucking now, I would remember this? Unsure and shaken, I returned to the festivities.

Chapter Two

*M*uch had changed for Liam Woods since the school yard days. The tall skinny build of his childhood had made way to a more muscular physique. He towered over most at six foot five, with broad shoulders and sculpted abs. He had long gotten rid of the glasses he had worn, allowing the world to see his soulful brown eyes. With a head full of thick dark hair, and the smile of a devil, he had become quite the ladies man over the years.

Long from the days in Sandy Bay, Liam had moved to the city of Winnipeg. Although never settling down, he had done well for himself and had even purchased a beautiful home in one of the city's most popular suburbs. He was content in his life and kept busy with his work, family, and friends. He had dated many women, but to no avail. None of them ever had captured his heart. A closet romantic, he kept holding out for that one love that could steal his heart and burn into his soul.

His father had been a police officer, and his father before him. It was in his blood to do the same. He had worked hard to achieve his position. After eight years of hard work, he had been asked to join the RCMP's Combined Forces Special Enforcement Unit, D Division. He was a proud and diligent worker. Together with his team, they had been most successful with the best arrest record of any unit in the country.

His work was what he poured his heart into. To him, every time he made an arrest, one less person got hurt or worse died. He had seen enough in his young life and as a constable to know the realness of the world. He had seen the coldness in the eyes of murders, boasting of their sins like conquests. Rapists who would laugh without remorse at the horrors they had brought onto others. To Liam, his co-workers and career were his guild in life, and he took it as seriously as a bullet to the face.

He had been on the squad for seven years before being promoted to unit project leader. The task at hand was to organize a squad that would specialize in the deconstruction of a few of the larger organized motorcycle gangs in the country. The two at the top of the list were the Devil's Cradle, and the God's Hammer motorcycle clubs. Liam's unit would be working closely with other provincial units on the same project. The teams would keep each other up-to-date on intel in their provinces as to track any large shipments of illegal arms, or drugs, being shipped across the provinces, and south to the American border.

He knew of the notorious Devil's Cradle club all too well. As he carried the file folder of surveillance pictures to the project room, memories of past events, far away from the office of the RCMP, flashed through his mind. The organization had held a strong presence in the small town he had grown up in. It was a bypass for the TransCanada highway and a perfect spot to hold power and control. His father had been an officer of the OPP. He had heard tid-bits of stories as a child, curiously listening through his father's closed den door.

He had started to pin up the pictures on the walls of the room, linking them by association. His mind floated back to earlier days of youth. He remembered Anny, another connection to the club. The small red headed girl he had spent most of his youth with, building forts and playing kissing tag. As he thought of the sweet girl with the sad eyes, he glanced down at the next picture to pin on the board, and saw them staring back at him. Anny, although grown and thinner, it was her with the same sad eyes starring off at something outside of the frame. As always she looked deep in thought. Beautiful and forlorn, there she was in his hand. Pinning her to the wall, his heart sank a little bit.

"Oh, Anny Omous. There's a story." A co-worker said while entering the room. "Her family is fucked. Some special kind of assholes they are."

"Yes. I am aware." Liam responded, hoping that would be the end of the conversation. He wasn't ready to divulge his full understanding of the family to a constable ranked beneath him.

"What her dad did, wow un-fucking believable. I can't believe she's affiliated with the club after that. She must be a fucking head case." The constable continued to carry on.

"Well, you never know. People sometimes just stay with what they know. Don't judge her too fast. She doesn't have a rap sheet and her Uncle is the vice president of the central Ontario chapter. She could just be around the clubhouse because of family." Liam says a bit harshly in retort.

"Read the file a bit further, boss. Her old man was patched in a few years back. Looks like, they're grooming him to rise through the ranks, and quickly. He's one mean son of a bitch. An enforcer of some type though we haven't been able to pin anything on him yet. He's definitely the last person you want knocking down your door. It's rumored he likes pinky fingers. Nice girl to be hanging out with a shit bag like that." With that, the constable sauntered out of the room.

Liam looked up at Anny's picture and stared at it for the longest time. His inner thoughts were trying to project through, to her. *Oh Anny, what the fuck have you got yourself into now?*

Chapter Three

My father had been the president of the Devil's Cradle motorcycle club's central Ontario chapter. His picture still hung on the wall in the clubhouse, even though he died when I was six. He was famous, well infamous to some, but in my world he was a legend. There were always stories of him outsmarting the cops, and beating the shit out of some asshole that had tried to screw the club. After his death, the vice president at the time assumed his role, and my Uncle Tom, assumed his. Tom had been in the chair ever since. Though only one of my three Uncles involved in the club, he was the most powerful. He was a burley man, with a scruffy beard, half way down his chest, full of silver and black hair. To most he was someone you never wanted to fuck with, but to me he was my teddy bear Uncle. He had always protected me, and took me under his wing when he had come into my life again at the age of eighteen.

My father, mother and brother Tom had died in a car crash. I was then given ward to my father's sister Maddilynn. She was a tough woman who took no shit, and raised me to be the same. From the little I could remember, we kept a quiet life in Sandy Bay. I finished school early, and graduated from college with an accounting degree by the time I was eighteen. It was around that time when I reunited with my Uncles. I had moved closer to the city for school, and somehow they found my address and started checking in on me. When I finished school I started working at the clubhouse. I was the book cooker, and boy did they need help in their kitchen. The previous accountant had been a bit of a tweaker, and had fucked things up royally. I saw him only once for a quick orientation when I first started working there. I didn't ask why his presence never graced the clubhouse again.

The work was good and I was being paid well. Plus I got to hang out with my family, and had been welcomed with open arms by the organization. It was family. My dad's reputation and my Uncle Tom made me some kind of quasi legacy. My dad had somehow saved the club from a major bust by the cops. The details were never fully shared, but I gathered he had taken out a rat. Whatever the details were it didn't matter, and I never asked. I was not in any way an actual member. I was kind of like a kid sister to everyone, and I was fine with that.

I had met Peter twelve years after starting my job. He had been a member of another club that ours had just acquired, and he was patched in immediately. He was medium build and burly. Clean shaven with a baby face, and bright green eyes, he didn't seem to match the others in the group. He was smart and cunning, his look giving him the edge he needed to get the better end of someone. No one expected him to be as tough as he was, with that sweet smile he could flash on in a moment's notice. At first, I didn't really take any interest in him. I had always been the hunter, and a good one to say the least. If I liked you, we were probably going to date. Peter was different. He sought after me, and it freaked me out a little bit. But after some coaxing, I gave him a shot.

It was a whirlwind first year. He was like no one I had ever met. He was crazy, overzealous, and quite frankly a bit of an asshole. Regardless, I fell for his charms and we were quickly living together. That first year we were inseparable. It seemed the world was ours for the taking. We thought we were unbreakable.

It had been a small Honda civic that had pulled out in front of us, on that fateful September day. We had been told that it was a godsend that it hadn't been a bigger vehicle. The bike had come to a dead stop when it careened into the car. I was thrown twenty-five feet through the air, and onto my back, on the other side of the vehicle. The impact had cracked my helmet clean in half, broken my pelvis, and dislocated my shoulder. I awoke in the hospital two weeks after the accident, to the amazement of the doctors on the ward.

Due to the head trauma, I was sent to a barrage of specialists, to identify any ongoing issues that would ensue after the injury. It was then, that the missing pieces from my past had come up for debate. The insurance company had been pushing for a speedy examination from the doctors. They had wanted to close the file, and be done with any compensation for the accident. I was healing quickly from the physical trauma, but the brain injury was still an issue being investigated. After months of specialist's visits, I had been told that I was suffering from a post-traumatic stress disorder. They had believed that though the accident had been traumatic, the extensive missing pieces of my memory from childhood most likely had been caused by previous psycho/social stress factors stemmed from my early years. I had repressed memories and the emotions attached to them. The accident, and the coma, had somehow prompted the disorder to be awakened. I could expect flashbacks, anxiety, and depression. The shrinks had described it as a volcano. The accident had caused the tectonic plates in my mind to shift and it would eventually erupt to expose the memories, and emotions, that my mind had locked away from me.

I was deemed unable to work. Peter had been filled with guilt over the whole thing, but it quickly grew to resentment. During the eight years after the accident, the light in his eyes had died. He had spent more and more time at the clubhouse, with his whores, and would rarely come home. His drinking had become intolerable. The times that he did grace me with his presence were scotch and anger filled. I learned to keep my distance. I had tried everything to make him happy, becoming subservient to his every need. Nothing seemed to work. I felt so guilty over something I had no control over. We had thought, and spoken, of breaking it off, but Peter couldn't live with the thought of leaving me ill. He had felt responsible, and would not be seen as the person who left me broken and defeated. I think more than anything, Peter was afraid of what my Uncle Tom may have done if he had left. We kept up appearances. Appearances were something very important to the club, and with Peter being as hungry as he was to advance, it became important to him as well. This had become our way of life, avoidance and personas. But something was bubbling up inside my mind. The lava from my volcano had been active. I could feel the winds of change from the deepest part of my psyche, rolling in a storm that would change everything I knew, and rock me to the very core.

Chapter Four

*I*t had been Tamara who had conned me into opening a
Facebook account. I had been in Sandy Bay for one of my bi-
yearly visits. A week spent rushing from one friend's house to
another. We had been drinking sangrias all day, sunning
ourselves, and by the time the evening rolled around we were

feeling no pain. Tamara was a beautiful woman. Stunning and confidant, she caught the eye of every man in the room. She had a prowess that most would kill for. We had been friends since grade school and she was always telling me stories of our childhood together. I looked to her as my personal historian.

She had been recalling her most recent story of a suitor's advances. I was engrossed in the details of the story, but her phone kept beeping. She was half distracted, checking her phone, and texting away. "Seriously girl, is that fucking thing attached to you when you sleep?" I asked her.

She laughed off the insult I had just thrown her way. I had never understood the draw to the whole Facebook thing. To me, if I didn't know you now, there was probably a reason why. I didn't see any purpose to share the intimate or non-intimate details of my life with people I really didn't even know. The club certainly would not have supported such actions. We were a private family, and our business was our business.

But in the mixture of drinks and laughter, and in such a different place than home, I was coerced by the charms of Tamara. Soon enough I had opened an account.

It had been an unusually hot August. The heat wave was in full swing for the second week in a row. I had found myself held up in our spare bedroom in the basement, seeking relief from the heat. I had covered the windows and was enjoying the darkness of the room. The last few months had been hard. I had found myself increasingly withdrawn, and my social anxiety was at an all time high. I had not visited the clubhouse in months. Peter hadn't been home in three weeks. He had been sent on a run to Victoria B.C. on club business. I was glad for the silence. I had felt solace in the darkness, like some old friend. Alone and bored, I decided to check my Facebook. I had been on a few times since opening the account. I had to keep calling Tamara to ask who the people sending friend requests to me were. She would laugh, and instruct as to who to say yes to, or who to ignore.

Scanning through the timeline, I found myself wondering how it felt to have a normal life. Pictures of happy families, and kids' birthday parties, were whizzing past my eyes. Such a different world than the one I knew. Suddenly a message box popped up.

"Hi. How are you? I haven't talked with you in forever." Said Liam

"Good and you?" I said trying to put a face to the name.

It had been so long since anyone had actually asked me how I was. I had segregated myself from most of my regular company. The few calls I had received from friends back home had been fuelled with drama over arguments with boyfriends. Rarely had the conversation turned to me and I was okay with that, not wanting to expose the depths to which I had allowed myself to sink. It had been unbelievably easy to talk with Liam. He had listened attentively to all of my responses. It was hard for me to tell him of my blackouts of my childhood. He had brought up events of our time together as children and I had to be honest with him. We had been talking for four hours when we decided to let each other go.

The entire evening had gone in a flash of laughter and good company.

It had been a week since the initial conversation with Liam. I had found myself ever drawn to him. It was strange. He had been so easy to talk to, and in our conversations it felt like home. Our talks continued in the coming months, and I could feel myself getting stronger. I had safe harbor with Liam. He was so different than anything I knew, and having someone completely out of my regular realm was amazing. No longer was I feeling the need to hide away in some dark corner of my mind. I was working hard trying to get healthy, and had even started to venture out to some of the club events. My days had become busy with schooling and my evenings were filled with conversation and light-heartedness with Liam. I looked forward to speaking with him, my heart missing a beat every time I would see a message on Facebook, or get a text. I felt like a schoolgirl. He had been trying to tease me with silly advances like: What are you wearing. I would always respond with some cheeky retort like, I'm wearing rubber boots and a moo moo, and shut him down. Somehow within our time together I was becoming whole again.

The club had been falling under strong scrutiny by the police, and everyone was on edge. Lips were to remain sealed on any issue with regards to the club. It was Christmas Eve, and I was still waiting for Peter at home. It had reached nine at night when I felt I'd had enough of waiting. Maddilynn was to arrive in the morning and be damned if we would spend another Christmas waiting on him to come home, only to be drunk and nasty. I decided to head to the clubhouse and get him myself.

Entering the compound, I could see the blinking Christmas lights through the window. The sound of AC DC was pouring over the parking lot through the building. Upon entering, I was met with a blast of pot and cigarette smoke. The party was in full swing. I scanned the room looking for Peter when I met eyes with my Uncle Tom. When he saw me, a look of panic spread across his face. He looked toward the back of the room where the stairs to the bunkhouse were. I knew what was going on right away. I ran across the room, before he could gather himself to stop me. I opened the door to the room with determination. The door slammed as it hit the wall. There stood Peter with a rode hard, put away wet, scooter trash whore attached to his dick. She was sucking his dick like it was a piece of gold. I ran across the room, pointing my finger at him, and screamed, "You son of a bitch! Are you fucking kidding me right now?"

Before I knew it, I could feel his hands around my windpipe. My momentum had changed, and I was moving backwards, faster than my feet could keep up. The impact of my body meeting the wall was so intense I could feel my ribs cracking. I could feel his hot scotch soaked breath on my face, as his grip on my neck tightened, cutting off my air supply.

"Who the fuck do you think you are? You fucking stupid bitch!" he screamed in my face, spit landing on my cheek. "If you ever talk to me like that again, I will fucking end you. Do you understand me?"

He was ripped off me suddenly. My Uncle Tom had made it to the room. He threw Peter off of me. I fell to my knees gasping for air. The drunken little bitch that had been making Peter's cock her own private meal suddenly spouted out. "Ya fuck you bitch! Get the fuck out of here!"

I lunged across the room, Uncle Tom catching me as I did. Still, I had managed to get her hair. I was pounding her in the head, when I felt my grip loosen. Peter was pulling her out of my grasp. I could feel my hands travelling down her legs, as we were being pulled apart. Fiercely holding on, my hands came across her feet. As we were pulling apart, I managed to get a hold of one of her cheap stilettos. From across the room she looked at me, hair all mangled and face full of blood. "Fuck you cunt!" she yelled, hopping mad, as Peter maintained his grip on her.
I hurled the shoe in my hand at her, hitting her square in the face." You ain't no Cinderella, bitch!" I screamed as my Uncle Tom tried to lead me out the door.

"You better fix this shit Peter!" I hear Uncle Tom say to Peter, in a don't fuck with me tone. With that, we were out of the clubhouse and in his truck. Heading to his house, I was fuming. I was done with this shit. I didn't care anymore. I decided right there and then that I would no longer be a doormat for Peter. I would spend my energy taking care of myself. If he wanted his whores so be it. I had Liam, and he was all and everything my heart could desire. I no longer would block his advances. I knew I wanted him, more than I had ever wanted anyone before.

"How are you holding up? You're pretty quiet over there, girl," my Uncle Tom questioned me in a soft tone.

Shifting my position, I felt a burning twinge through my ribs. "I'm here. My ribs are fucking killing me though." I said back, still looking out the window avoiding eye contact.

"Anny, what were you thinking running into the room like that? You know Peter has one hell of a temper. Don't you even think of telling your aunt Maddilynn. The last thing we need is more drama over this shit. We'll take a look at you ribs when we get to the house, and tape them if we have too. You'll have to wear a scarf or a turtleneck the next few days while she is here. I can see the bruises on your neck from here." He said, with a no buts about it attitude. "You and Peter are going to patch this up, and get over it quick. We've got too much happening right now in the ranks. The cops are being a real pain in the ass. We've been losing money everywhere, and they even pinched one of the new prospects. That little shit better not talk. This is for your ears only. The only reason I am sharing this with you is to stress the importance of appearances. We need to show a unified front right now, or the ranks will start to dissipate. That, my girl, is trouble, way more trouble than some bitch sucking your old man's cock. You get me?"

I nodded my head knowingly at him. I understood what he was saying even though I did not like it. *God, I had to be careful now. I couldn't even imagine what would happen if he found out I was talking with Liam.*

It was shortly after New Years that I had received word from Liam that he would be returning home for a holiday to Sandy Bay. It would be in February. He had organized an event to get together a group of friends that we had been in high school with together. I was ecstatic knowing that I would be seeing him. Our conversations had changed quickly after Christmas Eve, allowing his advances to go further. I was shocked at how easy it had been to speak to him of my desire. Smiling through the day, I found myself distracted by thoughts of Liam, imagining his hands on my body and his mouth on mine. Our conversations had become intense with passion and ever-more teasing. Liam had joked that he needed to drink a few beers for bravery in order to log onto his computer and talk with me in the evenings. I found it impossible that a man of his stature and physique would need courage to do anything he wanted to do. I was unable to control myself with him, and told him as much. He apologized and I told him not to. I said I liked it and he did as well. February had arrived soon enough, and I in a ball of nerves made the journey to Sandy Bay, knowing that the evening would prove to be a game-changer.

Chapter Five

L iam had known that the first time he had talked with Anny, his intentions were not good. He had thought it an excellent opportunity to acquire some intell on the club. Once engaged in conversation with Anny, he wasn't able to bring himself to do so. It took no time at all to remember who she had been to him all those years ago. Her quirky, twisted sense of humor made him smile. He found himself struggling with his guilt. His work had always come first but this time it would be his heart.

He had finally confessed to her that he was a cop during one of their first conversations. She had been taken aback and had pulled away a little from him. He had left out all of the details of his position, as to not have her run away completely, or have himself exposed to the club for that matter. They had made a deal, that she would not speak of anything about the club, and he of his work. She hadn't been speaking much about her life in the club anyway. Their conversations had a much deeper context than general day-to-day life. They were always talking of their dreams and desires. Anny had wanted to travel, and spoke in much detail of the places she had wanted to visit. She had decided that she was no longer going to accept her position in life, and that she would do her best to get back to some kind of work. She had even purchased a car she had been working on with a few of her friends, restoring it back to its original classic state. Liam was always encouraging her in any way he could. He liked that he could hear in her words that she was doing better. He found himself struggling with his loyalty to his guild.

Since their encounter at the restaurant, Liam had been making real strides in his investigation. Work had become busy, and he found himself spending more and more evenings working into the long hours of the night. He had missed talking as much with Anny, but every time he needed to see her, he would look up on the project room wall, and there she was. He hated that she hung there, a reminder of their masquerade. He had decided he wanted her picture down, and the only way that was going to happen was to get her old-man and her Uncle behind bars. Anny had told Liam of the incident on Christmas Eve. He had kept his cool when he spoke to her not wanting to rowel her up, but underneath it all his blood was boiling. He wanted a piece of this asshole and he was going to get it.

He was targeting the club and hard. His unit had already made sixteen arrests in the past few months. They had all been small-time players, but he knew eventually one of them would crack and lead them to a bigger fish. They had even picked up a young prospect from Ontario, who had been on his way back from Vancouver with a trunk full of heroin. They were connecting the dots quickly, but somehow the inner sanctum of the club always could elude them.

It was nearing the end of July, when he had received word from Anny that she intended to visit him. At first he had fought her on it, explaining how work had been busy, and how it wasn't a good idea for them to be seen together. As always, Anny had not allowed him to win. She didn't play fair, sending him photos of her boobs over his lunch break, and ever teasing him with her messages. He gave in. How could he not? Besides, he needed a break from work, and he wanted so badly to see her. It was set; she would be coming in August to see him. Everyday he would look at her picture and smile, awaiting their upcoming time together. Knowing that, he was in way over his head.

Chapter Six

*T*he time had finally arrived for my twenty-five-hour long drive to see Liam. My car was finally done, and the heat of the summer seemed to entice it to the road. I had carefully avoided much of the details of my holiday to Peter. Packing up the large trunk of the 69 Monty Carlo, I could feel his discontent with regards to my departure. The club had been involved in some shady dealings with a middle-man that had ties to a rival club. It had lead to a break down in some of the rival club's transportation of OxyContin from their west coast line. There had been talks of retaliation, and everyone was watching over their shoulders.

"You're picking a real shitty time to go." Peter said in a huff.

"It'll be fine. Quit worrying." I said back to him, trying to ease his tension. "Look, the car is in my name. No one has seen it at the clubhouse, so there's no heat there. Besides, what trouble can two middle aged women shopping at greenhouses get into? Stop worrying."

I had told him that I was visiting an old girlfriend, with plans of landscaping her backyard. He hadn't questioned it, and I left no room for speculation.

"Okay, well call me when you get there. Drive careful, and be safe. Oh and Anny, no speeding. The last thing we need right now is you on the cop's radar." He said, and pulled me in for a hug.

"I won't." I said, stepping into the vehicle. I just wanted to get out of there. I was already struggling with my mixed emotions of excitement to see Liam, and my guilt of lying to Peter.

As I turned out of the driveway I could no longer hold my excitement back. It was a beautiful sunny August day. I cranked my tunes, and allowed my mind to let go of any concerns of home. The warm wind was blowing my hair around like a storm of red. I was exhilarated. By the time I reached the outer limits of Thunder Bay, I was in need of some rest. I decided on a tourist station off the side of the highway. Quiet and deserted, the sky full of stars, a perfect place to refuel my energy. I pulled a tall can of beer and a blanket from my trunk. Spreading the blanket on the hood of the car, I laid there gazing at the beauty of the night. The low lights of the dash, glowing, from within the car, and the sweet sound of Bruce Springsteen's, "I'm on fire", playing softly in the background. I let my mind slip away. I felt free, alive, strong, and almost whole. After drinking up my beer and the feelings in my heart, I turned off the music, and crept away to sleep in the back seat of the car.

The morning sun was hot and it woke me from my sleep. I checked my phone for the time. *Six o'clock, not bad, a few hours sleep.* I needed to get back on the road. I still had a long drive ahead. After a good stretch, some clean clothes, and a quick morning maintenance routine I was off. The trip seemed to take no time at all, filled with thoughts of Liam. My heart was racing with images of his soft lips pressing down hard on mine, and his hands running the course of my body. It had been five months since our time spent thrust against the wall of the men's room, but I could still feel his hands still on my body, his breath on my neck, coaxing me to give into his every whim. I ran my fingers across my lips, recalling the bruising from his lips, and the sweetness of his mouth on mine.

Finally, I had arrived in Winnipeg. I stopped at a gas station not far from his house to freshen up. I texted Peter that I had arrived safe and sound. I had said that I would be busy for the evening and that I would talk to him tomorrow. *There, that should keep away any awkward phone calls.* Doing a double check in the mirror on exit, I felt confidant in my prowess. I could barely breathe pulling into his driveway. I shut off the car and checked my makeup in the rear view mirror. Taking a moment to calm myself, my inner voice was chanting at me, *Relax, you can do this. Relax just breathe.* I positioned my mirror back to its original state, and looked out the front window to see Liam standing on the front porch, grinning, looking down at me. I gave him a soft wave and tried to hide the shaking of my hands.

He, gorgeous as ever, was wearing a casual t-shirt and kaki shorts. The t-shirt, though loose, did nothing to hide his fit physique. The heat of the day had made him sweat, and a bit of breeze blew the shirt to hug his well-defined abs. The shirt sat teasingly, showing just enough for the imagination to run wild. His brown eyes sparkled, with a look that a lion gives a gazelle before attack, as I made my way up to him. He took my bag from my hands and opened the screen door, leading me into the house. We hadn't said a word to each other yet. The tension was so thick the air seemed to have weight. He dropped my bag on the floor and walked towards me. My body was tense and I could barely look him in the eyes. He pulled me into him close, his hand on the bottom of my back, leading me backwards like some naughty dance. My heart was pounding; my breath had quickened, as he stared down into my eyes like I was a meal to be had. I felt like I could jump right out of my skin. Just when I felt I couldn't take anymore of this taunting, I felt my knees bend forward from the seat of the couch against the back of them. In a blur of a moment he was on top of me. His lips were pressing down hard onto mine. Our hands, furiously pulling, and prying at each-others clothing. I could feel the heat of his naked chest on my breasts, moving up and down like the motion of the sea. He pulled at my jeans, kissing my feet, before yanking the legs of the pants clean off my body.

"Wait." I managed to say. "I need a shower. I slept in my car last night."

"Oh, we'll have a shower." He grins down at me. "But first let's get dirty!"

Hours later, after a lengthy couch, shower, and bedroom session, I lay warm and curled into Liam's body. Tented under the sheets I pressed my face into his chest, kissing it, and letting out a deep sigh into his skin. His arms squeezed me into him closer and he responded with a half awake groan. His long legs wrapped up in mine, like a rope not to be untangled. I could hear my phone going off for what seemed to be the hundredth time. Liams' had been beeping as well. Neither one of us had paid any attention; busy with much more important things that evening. The sun had started to rise and the room had a welcoming glow. I thought to myself that I could stay like this forever, tangled in his embrace, soft, safe, and warm. I could hear the coffee starting to brew. It must have been on a timer. I laid still tucked into him, not wanting to move, as he slowly started to stir. He pulled up the sheet and giggled at me.

"What are you doing down there? Is this your private fort?" He said looking down at me.

"Yep !" I reply. "Private members only." I giggle back at him.

I crawled up and leaned in for a soft morning kiss.

"I guess we have to leave the bed sometime right?" He said, "You must be starving. Let's make some breakfast and see who the hell won't leave us alone."

"Okay." I say, with a pout of a child whose toys have been taken away. I could have stayed there all day.

I sat up and scanned the floor for something to wear. I found a t- shirt of Liam's and threw it on. In the living room I inspected my phone. Liam was already scanning his as he waited for the coffee to finish. *Twelve messages! What the fuck?* As I made my way through them I felt my stomach turn.

"Liam, I gotta go," I said to him in shock.

Looking up from his phone with worry he answers, "I know. I'm so sorry Anny."

Chapter Seven

I pushed the gas peddle down to the floor as far as it would go, the 69 Monty Carlo, responding well to the tireless pursuit of home. My mind was racing with thoughts of Peter, who lay in the ICU ward of Toronto General Hospital. Guilt rushed over me. *What if he didn't make it? Oh God, what if he died while I was away satisfying my own selfish needs.*

Tears welled up in my eyes. I swerved trying to see the road. Thoughts of my Uncle Tom were rolling through my mind. They had killed him. The mother fuckers had shot him, right in front of his own house. The rival club, known as the God's Hammer, had taken their revenge. Peter had been with him and had been shot as well. Uncle Tom had died right away. Peter had been rushed to the hospital, and last I knew he was in surgery.

I could feel my anger boiling in my blood. I hated this life. The blood and violence had become a constant factor in club business. I was done with it. Please, God, let Peter live, was all I could think, as I pushed the car to her limits. I didn't care about a speeding ticket. *Fuck the cops. Oh ya, you just did.* My inner voice reminded me.

My mind shifted to the half rushed conversation with Liam as I was getting ready to leave. His words ripped through my heart and head.

"We can't do this anymore Anny. It's too dangerous. Do you see what just happened here? Everything is different now. If they knew where you were, you would be dead in a day. Do you understand that? Do you? And me I could lose my job or worse be up on charges with a target on my back from your family. This has to stop. We need to cool this for a while. No more calling, texting, or Facebook. You understand me Anny? You understand me?"

The words were screaming in my head. Yes, I understood. I didn't want to, but I did. I had created a bullshit scenario again, like always. My heart was broke with the thought that Liam and I were done. My head was screaming at me. *You should know better. Look what you have done.*

I made the twenty-five hour trip in eighteen hours. I had no idea how I wasn't pulled over, and I had completely blacked out the last three hours of the trip. Running through the hospital, nearly knocking over a few people along the way, I made it to the unit where Peter was. I came to a screeching stop, almost passing the waiting room filled with clubhouse members and wives. My aunt Maddilynn jumped from her seat, tears in her eyes, and rushed to hug me. Balling on my shoulder, she tightened her hug.

"What's going on with Peter? Is he out of surgery? Is he gonna be okay?" I berated her with questions. She composed herself and answered, "Yes, the doctor said he's going to make it. It will be a bit of a recovery, but he's going to be fine. Uncle Tom," She started to say and broke down again into tears. I sat her down on one of the waiting room chairs and held her. Rocking her back and forth to sooth her pain, I whispered, "I know. I know. It's going to be okay. It's going to be okay."

The funeral was a tapestry of shiny exhaust pipes rumbling and patched up jackets as far as the eye could see. The news of my Uncle's death had made its way to the front page of most of the nation's papers. The police were even present for escort, and to keep the reporters at bay. Uncle Tom's casket had been brought to the graveyard in style, being towed behind a trike, in a glass trailer, donned as the last ride. In tail were over one hundred and fifty motorcycles and numerous amounts of other vehicles. It was a good service, sweet and sad all at once. The colours of the fall leaves gave a beautiful back drop to the whole grim affair.

The club was in a state of transition and you could feel the buzz in the crowd. Uncle Tom had been vice president and someone would be voted in soon to replace him. The rumour was that Peter was being considered for the position. Though fresh out of the hospital, he was healing quickly. Anger had been fuelling his recovery. Young-blood, mixed with ideas for a smart retaliation, was considered invaluable by the club at the time. The police had an ever-watchful eye on the clubhouse and it's membership.

I had distanced myself from everything involving the club, except for Peter. The warning, from Liam was always scratching at the back of my brain. *Keep quiet about all this Anny, and whatever you do, stay away from anything to do with the club.* I had been aiding Peter with his recovery. Now that he was much more mobile, I had started back to work. I had gotten a job with an airline, working as a stewardess. I loved it. It afforded me my much needed time away from home, and allowed me to travel. There was something about being up in the air, hurling toward some foreign destination that seemed so enticing. The job allowed for cheap flights for me, and I visited back to Sandy Bay more often to see friends.

Over the next seven months or so, I could feel myself coming into my own. I had been planning a year or so long trip with my girlfriend Cassy. We would explore Africa, Malaysia, and Asia. We had been researching different volunteer organizations, and had found some exotic locations to explore. Cassy was a fun, beautiful, and charismatic woman. Her job would allow for a year and a half sabbatical, without worry of being bumped down the seniority list. She had brought up the idea, and I immediately had fell in love with it.

We worked diligently at the planning process, and the stacks of paper work, in order to have everything ready for our mid-April departure date.

Everything was changing so quickly. Peter was being groomed for his rise up the ranks at the club. He had been so busy, and with my work schedule, we had barely even seen each other in a month. We had been doing alright, just walking through the paces. I had resigned myself to the fact that we were best suited for each other, regardless of the lack of love. I knew he had a few chicks on the side, and I didn't even care anymore. I had Africa. I had become more outgoing and comfortable in my own skin. I had even spent the time and money to get a full back tattoo that I had always wanted. It was beautiful - A tree of life, the trunk twisting up the length of my back and roots curling downward towards my ass. The branches were only slightly filled in, leaving room for colourful flowers, marking locations I had been, to be drawn in later. *Boy was I gonna fill that tree.* Everything had been slowly calming down since Tom's death. As promised, I hadn't spoken to

Liam. Though I thought of him often, I pushed him to the back of my mind.

It was supper time, two and a half weeks before I was to leave, when I got the call that my friend Sara had died. She had succumbed to ovarian cancer and died quickly during the night. Making my phone calls to work and to friends, I planned for the trip to Sault St. Marie. The funeral would be that coming Saturday.

The funeral was put together well. It hadn't dragged on like some I had been to. The company of old friends helped through the sadness of the affair. I hadn't seen many of them since the reunion so long ago. Scanning through the pictures of Sara on the boards in the foyer, it hit me hard. She was so young. This could happen to any of us. One day you are just living your life, trying to make the best of it, then bam it's over just like that. Then I saw the picture from our reunion. Sara was smiling so happily, everyone looking a little younger, and a little drunk. My eyes looked across the photo and stopped on a familiar face that was always in my head. Liam. So handsome, so tall, I missed him too much for words to say. It was there, looking at his face, when all the feelings I had for him came rushing back like a freight train through my heart.

"Hey Anny! You coming?" I heard Tamara call to me from across the room.
I took one last long look at the picture, and placed it back down on the table." Ya, I'm coming. Wait up." I shouted over to her.

We had decided to get rip roaring drunk, at a restaurant close to the hotel we were all staying at. The hotel was close to the airport, which made it convenient for us that were flying out the next day. We all sat at the bar, doing shot after shot, and telling stories about good times with Sara. The last thing I remember was pouring the last shot of Jägermeister, emptying the bottle into my shot glass. A blur of events followed.

I woke up. My head was pounding and so heavy I could barely lift it. *Holy shit I had drank way too much.* My eyes were burning as I tried to open them. *I must have left the curtains open in the room before passing out.* As my eyes adjusted to the light and focused in, I started to panic. I jumped up to a sitting position and let out a long groan. I had moved way too fast, too quickly, for my head to handle. I was holding my face in my hands, until I could lift my head again, when I realized I was naked. *OH FUCK! WHAT HAPPENED? WHERE AM I?* I felt the bed move from someone stirring behind me. I turned slowly as if not to startle a rabid animal. *This was gonna be bad.* I lifted the sheet covering the person's face, still debating whether to look or just run. Big brown eyes looked back at me. I gasped and dropped the sheet back down, covering his face.

"Good morning sunshine." Liam said, a little muffled from the sheet covering his mouth.
I laid back down and covered my head with the pillow, trying to retrace my steps from the night before.
"Have some questions do you?" he needled me.

"Yes," I said weakly from under my hiding spot.

"Good, me too." he said back, as he moved over to cuddle me.

"Hey you're wearing pajamas. Did we have sex?" I asked him.

"No." He said, not offering anymore.

"Then why am I naked?" I ask.

"Because you puked and some got on you." He laughed at me.

"OH MY GOD!" I groaned. "Wait, that explains the pants and shirt but why am I NAKED?" He shot me a devilish grin. "I love this! When did you get it?' he said, running his fingers up the outline of my tattoo and avoiding my question. I threw my pillow at him and hit him in the face. "You jerk." I laughed.

"Come on, let's get something to drink into to you. I may even have some Jagermeister if you want," he teased me, pulling at my hand.

"Blah, you're gonna make me sick again," I teased back, curling tighter into a ball, as not to be tugged out of bed.

"Come on, up and at 'em. I'll make you breakfast and then you can have a bath." He said, as he ripped the covers off me, and gave my ass a hard slap. "There's a t-shirt and boxers in the dresser you can wear while we wash you clothes."

"Man, you're bossy in the morning, officer!" I shout out after him.

I pulled myself up and made my way to the dresser. I threw on a t-shirt and boxers, as I was requested to do, and shuffled my feet to the open living room/kitchen area. Plunking myself down on a stool, I gave him a sheepish grin. He had already made me a coffee, and had started on the grease-filled breakfast. He proceeded to tell me of the known events of the prior evening. Somehow, in my drunken stupor, I had managed to make my way to the airport, and hop on a flight. He was awoken by pounding on his door at three in the morning. The cabby had made sure that someone had answered, and had wished him a good luck to the rest of the evening's ensuing events. Liam laughed as he described my crazy ranting about some picture and how we were all going to die soon. We finished our breakfast and he went to draw me a bath. I checked my phone. Whew, only one message, Tamara asking if I had made an earlier flight. I responded back yes, glad she had already given me a cover story.

"It's ready." Liam called from the bathroom.

In the bathroom, I brushed my teeth, disrobed, and slipped into the warm tub full of bubbles. Liam sat on a chair watching as I teasingly washed myself.

"There's room for one more in here, you know," I said softly to him.

I could see his mind starting to contemplate the offer.

"Anny, we gotta talk." He said, his tone growing serious.

I turned myself in the tub on my stomach, and leaned my arms over the side, facing him. He sounded so serious. I wanted to give him my full attention.

"Okay." I answered back.

"I met someone. We've been seeing each other for a while now. It's kind of getting serious." He said quietly.

My heart dropped into my stomach.

"Okay," I respond. "Who is she?"

"Her name is Amber. We met through work. She's an administrator." He answered back.

"Oh, that's great. I'm happy for you." I say, trying hard not to sound disappointed. *How could I be? He was single, and I was unavailable. This was so fucked up!*
He could see the disappointment in my eyes. "This will have to be the last time this happens. We cannot keep doing this, you understand me?" He said, shooting me a grin. "Apparently I can't control myself around you either."

My eyes lit up. He undressed and climbed into the soapy water to join me. The water splashed from the sides of the tub, as he sat down behind me. I leaned back into his body and relaxed. We sat enjoying the warmth of the water and each other's company, playing with each others fingers and the curves of each other's body.

"Do you really have no memories from your childhood?" He suddenly asked.

"No, not anything." I answer. "Why?"

"Uh, it's just so strange," he said in quiet voice.

"What do you mean? Why are you asking about this, anyway?" I turned to look at him as I asked.

"No, I didn't mean anything by it. It's just such a big period to not remember anything. It's kinda sad is all," he said, looking distracted.

"Yeah, I guess, but I really wouldn't know the difference. I've always been this way," I answered.

He leaned down and kissed me softly. A long deep kiss that seemed to have lasted forever.

"Come on, your cab will be here soon to take you to the airport," he said.

And with that, sadness fell over the rest of our time together. Packing up my things, it hit me: This would be the last time I would see Liam. I could feel a sharp pain in my heart and a lump in my throat as I kissed him goodbye and got into the cab. My heart was in mourning. Mourning a love it would never be able to have.

Chapter Eight

I had arrived home in the early hours of Monday morning. My head hit the pillow like a ton of bricks. Sleep was all I could think about doing. I had to be at work the rest of the week, Friday being my last day with the airline. I had made sure that I had a good week to finish wrapping up any loose ends, before taking off for over a year. I hadn't seen or spoken to Peter since before I had left, and I was relieved to find the bed was empty. I stretched out, thankful that I would not have to answer questions about my time away.

The rest of the week went by in a blink of an eye. I had gone for a quick goodbye drink with some of the girls from work on the Friday evening. As my cab pulled into the driveway at home, I knew what I was in for. There must have been twenty bikes in the yard. There were people drunk and passed out on the lawn, and the music was cranked. I paid the cabby as fast as I could and walked up to the house. *Great! Just fucking great!* I thought to myself, *as I pushed open the front door. Just what I was hoping for: a quiet night after work.*

As I entered the house I heard Peter bellow from across the room, "Baby!!"

"Hey!" I said, trying to act happy and surprised. He was wrecked, along with the house.

He flew across the room, picked me up, and spun me around. Everyone in the room was laughing and singing.

"Guess what, baby?" He said proudly. "You're looking at the new VP."

"That's great, babe. I'm happy for you," I said back. Feigning tiredness, I pretended to yawn.

"What am I fucking boring you?" He snarled.

Great, he's getting nasty, right on time, I thought to myself.

"No, I'm just exhausted from this week, work and Sara's funeral. I didn't know you would be home or I would have rested up for you," I said sweetly, to avoid any further anger from him.

"I'm gonna lay down for a while okay. I'll get up in a bit and have a beer with you all."

"Okay baby." He slurred back, "Hey, before I forget to tell you, there's a special dinner at the clubhouse tomorrow. Make sure to cancel any plans you may have."

"Okay," I said back, as I hurried up the stairs away from the party, knowing full well I wasn't going to return.

The next morning I woke up to the sound of bikes starting up. Good, some of them were leaving. Most times the morning coffee would be a morning beer, and the party would start all over again. I was in no mood for that today. I just wanted to get through this week with no bullshit, and get gone. The house was a write-off, and I spent the first two hours of the morning just trying to get the kitchen back together so I could make breakfast. I was not impressed. Peter was snoring on the couch, beer still in hand. I took a good look around at the disaster that was everywhere and decided to say fuck it. *This was not my problem anymore. Let him clean this shit up.* I thought to myself.

I decided to go for a run and get away from the house. I needed to clear my head. *One more week,* I kept telling myself, over, and over again: *One more week and freedom.* I cranked up my tunes and ran hard. It must have been an hour before I made it back to the house. Stopping to catch my breath and walking out my burning muscles, I noticed that all the bikes were gone, including Peter's. *That's odd.* I thought. *Oh well, better for me.*

In the house, not much had changed from when I had left. Only the vacancy of our house guests, and a note from Peter on the fridge had differed. His note was a reminder to me about the party at one o'clock that day. He had asked that I dress nice, and if I wouldn't mind cleaning up a bit. *FUCK YOU* My inner voice screamed. I wasn't going to clean up any of this shit. I headed for the shower and got ready for the big party.

I pulled into the clubhouse ten minutes later than was requested that I arrive. It was my little fuck-you to Peter. I was still fuming from his note. Surprisingly, I was met with a smile. He seemed oddly loving and happy, and it was weirding me out a bit. Peter escorted me to a long table and cracked me a beer. Everyone was there. There must have been a hundred people. I hadn't been there in so long. There were many people I didn't even recognize. There seemed to be a few new old ladies, and a few new prospects. Though it was nice to see and talk with everyone, I felt tired of the scene. Everyone was giving me condolences for my Uncle Tom and that was a subject I did not want to broach. With the food finally ready I was happy to eat, hoping we would leave shortly thereafter.

Peter had been acting strange. He was touching me constantly, even holding my hand at times. This was not the Peter I knew. We never held hands, and we were not touchy feely. The truth was, we hadn't even had sex since I had caught him with the little scooter trash tramp over a year ago. Part way through the dinner, he leaned close to me and whispered in my ear "You know I love you, right?"
I stopped eating, and looked at him puzzled. He stood up and started hitting his fork off his beer, making a clanging sound, to gather the crowd's attention.

"Attention all you fuckers." He yelled loudly, the crowd laughing back in response.
"You know that I have been with this lovely lady here for almost ten years now. Well today, in front of all of you, her family, her friends, and her community, I want to ask her a

very special question." And with that, he dropped to his knees, pulled out a ring, and said. "Babe will you make me an honest man and marry me?"

I sat paralyzed. I couldn't move. I couldn't breathe.

"Anny, will you?" He said again, looking hard at me for a response.

All at once, the only thing I could think to do was run. I jumped up and sprinted to my car. I could hear the voices behind me buzzing, and Peter yelling after me shouting my name. My hands where shaking as I tried to get the keys into the ignition. Finally I managed to get them in. *Hurry Anny, hurry!* My inner voice was screaming. I could see Peter running to the car. I got it started. I could hear the clutch grind as I slammed it into reverse.

"Anny what are you doing?" Peter was yelling, still running, trying to catch up with the car. I slammed the brake, threw it into first gear, and slammed on the gas. I could see Peter in my rear view mirror waving his arms for me to stop. But I couldn't stop. I put it into second gear, the engine winding out, then third, and fourth. Finally I realized I had to slow down. I was panicked. *What the hell was that? Marriage, was he insane? Was I? I did just run away like a crazy person from everyone and everything I knew at a hundred miles an hour.* It didn't matter anymore. I was driving and I wasn't going to stop. I knew where I was going. For the only thought besides running that came to mind in that second he asked me, was that of Liam.

I had driven straight through to Winnipeg, the third trip there in a year. I was a force to be reckoned with. Crazied, and stopping only for gas and coffee, I was in a zone. I was telling Liam once and for all what I thought, and what I felt. I had turned my phone off. It had been buzzing nonstop. When I reached the gas station near Liam's house to fill up, I turned on my phone to call him. As soon as I did, it rang. It was Peter. Amped full of courage and coffee I answered.

"Anny what the fuck is going on? Where are you? Why did you leave?" He questioned, getting angrier by the second." You embarrassed the fuck out of me, you know? You made me look like an asshole in front of everyone."

"That's right, always about you, huh? Well guess what! You made yourself look like an asshole all on your own. Marry you? Are you insane? Why, to make you look better to the club. You trying to fill my daddy's shoes or something?" I retort, yelling into the phone.

"Watch your tone you fucking bitch." He snarled back. "We've been together ten years. Ten fucking years! Does that loyalty mean nothing to you, or are you just an ungrateful fucking cunt?"

"Yes, ten years Peter. Ten years of feeling inadequate and tolerated. I gave you my thirties. Like fuck I'm giving you my forties too. You know what I've learned Peter? Do you? Maybe you're the one who's inadequate, and I can't tolerate you any longer." I hung up the phone and realised that I had been screaming. The entire block was staring at me. One woman started to clap. *Great, like I needed more people knowing my business.*

I paid the man inside for the gas and sped off in a hurry. My mind, tired from the drive and angry from the call from

Peter, fooled me into some wrong turns. After twenty-five minutes I realized I was lost. I pulled into the nearest parking lot I could find.

I picked up the phone and called Liam's cell. He answered after two rings.

"Hello." he said. I could hear people in the background.

"Liam it's me. I'm here. I need to talk to you right now, but I got turned around. I've been driving for like twenty-five minutes past that gas station and..."

"Anny, slow down. What are you talking about?" he says, concerned.

"I left him. I need to see you. I need to talk to you. I'm lost. I'm in some fucking mall parking lot like twenty-five minutes from the gas station by your house. How do I get to your place?" I said sounding defeated.

I could hear the sound of the crowd behind him fade slowly, as he found a more private place to talk.

"You can't come here Anny. I've got like twenty RCMP here for a barbeque. They'd know who you were in a second. I know where you are. Sit tight. I'll find a reason to get out of here to come see you," he said, and hung up the phone.

The parking lot was empty, being supper time on a Sunday. I sat quiet, staring out the windshield, going over the events of the last few years in my mind. It was dusk when I saw the headlights of his suburban pulling into the parking lot. I flashed my head lights and he followed my que, parking next to my car. I opened my door and stepped out. He did the same, looking in disbelief to see me.

"He asked me to marry him Liam. In front of everyone, he asked me to marry him. I couldn't. I just couldn't. All I could think about was you," I said, shaking my head and looking at my feet.

"Anny. there's," he started to say when I cut him off.

"I want you, just you, all and everything about you. I'm done with that life. I promise it's over. We can do this, right?" I said, looking into his eyes, tears starting to well up.

The blood had drained from Liam's face, and he was pale as a ghost.

"Anny, Amber said yes. I didn't want to tell you. I asked her before you came from Sara's funeral. You were going away. I didn't want to hurt you. I just, I just can't," he said, almost whispering.

My heart stopped dead in my chest. I could feel the pain all the way down to my toes.

"When?" I asked, piercing my lips to keep from screaming *NO!*

"Next year, in June." He answered.

I started pacing like a dog in heat. I could feel my blood pressure rising.

"Anny, come on! Don't do this!" he said.

"Do you love me?" I asked him.

"Anny, stop! Stop this right now! We could never be together, outside of what we had. You know this! It doesn't matter if you leave that life. It will always be apart of who you are, and who you were. We can't be together!" he said, getting agitated.

"No, you tell me you don't love me right now!" I said aggressively.

He looked to the ground and said nothing.

"Tell me right now that you don't love me, and I will never see you again!" I said, raising my voice.

He looked me dead in the eyes and said nothing. I could see the tears burning in them.

I pushed him, crying, and screamed, "Tell me!!"

He grabbed my arms and pushed me away from him. He opened the truck door. He gave me a pained look, biting his bottom lip as if to hold the tears in his eyes. For a moment, he looked like he wanted to say something, but he didn't. He simply stepped into the vehicle, started it, and drove away.

Chapter Nine

*T*he twenty- two and a half hour flight from Toronto to Rabat, Morocco was welcoming. It gave me a chance to digest some of the most recent events. The fiasco with Liam had left me rattled. Poor Peter was beside himself, when I returned home. I had all intentions of leaving him, but after a six-hour long conversation full of tears and truths, we decided that this year apart would do us well. I would continue on my path of self discovery, and he on his own. We agreed that when I returned, we would make our decision on our future then. I had decided this was a golden opportunity to distance myself from both of them. Liam had made his choice, and apparently he didn't want, or need, me in that capacity. He was right. How could we make it work? We were just too different. Now with my adventure on the way, I decided no more Facebook. That shouldn't be too hard of a task, considering the majority of our planned destinations. The next available WiFi was in Bali, and that was three months away from now. As the tires hit the landing strip, I could feel all my worries of Canada float away.

Morocco was amazing. The sights, smells, and colours were almost overwhelming. Cassy and I had gotten jobs, teaching French to children at the Dar Attaliba (house of female students) in Rabat's east end. We had arrived just in time for the cooler temperatures of the Mediterranean climate to kick in. Thank God, as it was still so hot. I didn't know how the Muslim ladies could keep so wrapped up, and not pass out. Our lodging was with a home-stay family. Although their main language was Arabic, we were able to communicate with broken French, and many a laugh was had over dinners of Tangine, (a spicy Moroccan stew). In the evenings, Cassy and I would drink mint tea and listen to the sounds of the city around us, drinking it in as well. After two weeks we packed our bags, thanked our hosts, and were off to Ghana.

We landed in Accura the capital in the south, and after meeting our program official, we were quickly whisked away to a small rural village near Awaso. It was the rainy season, and the difference between Morocco and the tropical humid heat was astounding. The average daily temperature was twenty-seven degrees. We were placed in a volunteer housing unit, six to a room, on bunk beds. It was a little rough, but at least there were western style toilets. The cold showers were kind of welcoming in the heat. Everyday was a challenge in the rain, working construction, but we got quit a bit accomplished on a local medical clinic. The people of the village were kind and their children sweet. They would feed us Fufu and Banku, a local staple.

By the time we landed in Cape Town, South Africa, I was coming into my own, no longer being haunted by my actions of the last few years. The month so far had been so enlightening. I had been practicing my photography skills like mad. I was even taking pictures, with messages to make videos, for friends on our return. I was happy and Cassy was seemingly so as well. We had arrived at the end of May. The cooler air was a relief. Some days, it didn't reach over fifteen degrees. We were working, assisting teachers, at one of the two schools in the community of Muizenberg. Cassy was at one, and I the other. The community was a safe suburb of Cape Town, about a forty to fifty minute drive to the town's centre. We stayed in a volunteer housing unit. The unit was huge compared to the previous one we had stayed in. It needed to be. This time we were surrounded by forty-five other volunteers, people from all over the world. The evenings were so full of stories being shared; it only fuelled my travel bug further. As our two weeks closed in, my journal full of new friends' e-mail addresses and phone numbers, I was excited for our next two destinations.

The flight to Nosey Be, Madagascar was sketchy at best. I'm pretty sure the pilot had gotten his license online. But we arrived unscathed all the same.   The adventure of the trip there was only compounded by the absolute surreal majesty of the island itself. We were heading to the island of Nosey Kumba, a few kilometers away by boat, a twenty-minute ride. We were lucky to have both been placed on this project together. The program only brought up to six volunteers for a three-week period. We were to be working, recording data, with regards to forest conservation. There were many species of wildlife that had been pushed to near extinction there due to deforestation. We would trap, release, and gather information on many of theses animals. I was beside myself to see a lemur. Next to sloths, they were my favorite animal. We slept in locally built huts, all six of us. The close quarters were something to get used to, but for the experience it was worth it. I felt like some ancient explorer or biologist. Sometimes I would pretend I was never going home. The tranquility of the nature, and the pureness of the forest, touched my soul. It was a sad day on departure, but I knew our next location was sure to bring about the same feelings of awe and wonderment.

Victoria Falls, Zimbabwe - this was the Africa you see in the movies. We were heading to a private game reserve in the province of Matabeleland, close to the Zambia border. The reserve was located in the popular touristy town of Victoria Falls. We would be working doing more duties for assisting in wildlife conservation again, but this time we were going to see some lions! Originally the protection zone was constructed for the critically endangered black rhino, but the other big four on that list, lions, leopards, elephants and buffalo fell under the protection of the reserve as well. The lodging was within the compound. We were safe, with twenty-four hour armed security guards, and an electric fence, to keep any of the big predators out of our camp. Finally: private rooms. Nothing fancy: single bed, a desk, dresser, ceiling fan and privacy. There was even a swimming pool, and hot showers. I didn't think anything would top Nosey Kumba, but this took the fucking cake. The first time you see a lion look at you, you know your grain, an experience not ever to be forgotten. The days flew by too quickly, and we prepared for our travels to our last two stops on the continent.

The Kilimanjaro Airport in Tanzania was insane. The whole city seemed to thrive on chaos. The hustle-bustle and loudness of it all made me glad we were headed somewhere a little less haywire. The roads on the way to Arusha were bad. The rainy season had just ended, and I had never experienced potholes of that significance in my life. Once in Arusha, we were divided up, and sent on another short trip to the local rural villages. Cassy and I would be separated on this adventure. I didn't mind. I could handle my own. I could tell she was a little nervous though. She was headed to work with people with HIV, and I to work with some little ones at an orphanage. The surge in HIV had meant many young children were orphaned, left to live alone, and to suffer the same fate as their parents. I was surprised to find that the majority of the children did not live there and would come for just a few hours a day to participate in some schooling, and to have a meal. The children were so strong. One day after feeding some of the babies, I wandered out to the front wrap-around porch. The day was cloudy and hazy. I heard something behind me. I turned to see Tuta, a sweet doe-eyed girl, sitting quietly, watching me. I walked over and sat with her. She reached out and grabbed my hand, looking up at me with her big brown eyes. I could see it in her, and she in me. We shared the same pain. I was around her age when I lost my parents. A car accident I was told by my adoptive aunt. Even though I couldn't remember them, I could still feel them. In that moment something in me shifted. That brief moment in time, holding the girl's hand, her pain reflecting into mine, would turn out to be a definitive one.

Our last stop in Africa was Nairobi, Kenya. Once again we would be separated for work, but at least we were lodged together at a local family homestead. Cassy's job would be assisting in teaching, and I with a group that would travel to Kibera, the largest slum in Africa, to aid in women's support. We travelled with guards, and would do house calls to women in need or in transition with families. Most of the women had HIV to only further their harsh reality. Most were abused, and poverty stricken. It seemed hopeless to try and be optimistic for their futures. There were days, though, that we would meet in a local community building in Nairobi and aid the women in an variety of crafting skills; training was what it had been coined. The women would then have wares to sell at the market. There was sadness through it all that resonated in me like some dark and twisty familiarity to theses women and their pain. I didn't like it.

In the evenings, I appreciated the bubbly chatter of Cassy, sharing her stories from her present and previous jobs. It was a welcome distraction. Since the orphanage, I had found myself slipping inward. It was like an itch I needed to scratch in my brain, but couldn't. Something just edging in, and it reminded me of the feelings I had run from. I had been at such peace so far on this trip. Why was this starting again? I had been having flashbacks. Nothing was recognizable, but smells, sounds, and strange images. The shrinks back in Canada had given up. They had told me that maybe whatever was locked away needed to stay there for now. They had assured me that when I was ready the memories would come. I did not want this to be now. The evenings were harder, and that's why I was so glad for Cassy's bubbly personality. At least we were heading for Bali next. We had splurged and upgraded our lodging. A little luxury was needed after these past three months or so. Everything would be better there. I just had to keep in whatever was trying to slip out of my darkness. Bali will be great! I told myself, a little worried that I was lying, and I knew it.

Chapter Ten

We arrived in Bali in July, during the hot dry season, a day earlier then our orientation, to settle in and relax. We had splurged, and instead of the regular volunteer housing were able to find lodging at a guest house of one of the locals in the village. They had come recommended, and had passed all the scrutiny of the agency we were working for. We each had our own rooms with a double bed, and a big ceiling fan made of bamboo, the blades cut into shapes of leaves. There was a terrace that overlooked a lush, beautiful garden, and a swimming pool we could use. That was going to come in handy in the heat. The very best of course was air conditioning, and WiFi. We were however warned that it would not be high speed. Regardless, in the midst of this adventure, some resemblance of home was welcoming. We would be there for three glorious weeks, before heading to Thailand. We were going to suck up every minute of it. We would be working on the island of Nusa Penida, a forty-five minute boat ride from Sanhur. Very few of the natives of the island spoke English or French, just their native tongue of Indonesia Ruphia. We would defiantly become immersed in this adventure. The role of work on the island would be turtle conservation. We would feed and care for sick and injured turtles, along with assisting some of their eggs to hatch. The island was incredible.

In the evenings after our swim, we would eat traditional food prepared by our hosts. A barrage of flavours from Sate Aymen, (chicken or pork skewers with sate), Mei Goreng (fried noodles and vegetables), and my favourite Gado Gado, (mixed vegetables with sate sauce). No matter what we received, it was always good and we were sated. Evenings were relaxing, looking out over the gardens, laughing over wine and stories. Cassy never asked about Peter, and I never said a word about him. She was good that way, never prying. She did not know about Liam, nor did anyone else. I couldn't explain without exposing him. So I kept that all locked up. She respected that, even though I could see she was curious.

Bedtime was the hardest for me with the darkness trying to scratch its way out. Blurred dreams were an ongoing occurrence. I refused to go on Facebook, the one past time I had used when restless nights were a part of my routine. I couldn't bare to see pictures of Liam and his fiancée, spread across my screen like salt in a wound. Surely by now the wedding invites or event organization had started. Not that I would be receiving one. No, I would not torture myself that way. My mind was already trying to break, and I had no time for my heart to as well. So I would lie in bed with my thoughts, and always they would turn to Liam.

The clash of thunder awoke me from my half sleep. I shot up shaking and crying. My sheets were soaked with sweat. I couldn't control my breathing. Panicking, I tried to get out of my bed, and fell to the floor. I curled up into a ball in the corner of the room, trying to process the series of events that my mind had spilled out for me to see. Rocking back and forth, I recalled my flashback.

A crack of what I thought was thunder, followed by screaming, awoke a six year old me from my sleep. Stumbling from my bed, bare foot and in a nighty, I made my way to the hallway on the upper floor. I could see a light on down the stairs through the railing. I tip toed across the landing, and slipped in something warm and wet. It looked black in the dark, and it was sticky. I looked ahead to see the crumpled-over body of my brother Tom. He looked at me and whispered, "Run." I looked at him, frozen like a deer in head lights.

"Run now Anny," he whispered a little louder.

    I could hear whimpering from my mother down in the lit up room, and a soft pact pacting sound. I made my way down the flight of stairs as quiet as a mouse. As I reached the bottom of the stairs, I was drawn towards the sound. I could see a man on top of my mother. Her face was red with blood, and almost unrecognizable. I could see her; see me, though the blood was running into her eyes. The man was continuously hitting her. The light flickering off the blade of the knife where it was not crimson stained.

    "No, Anny. No." she mustered, throat gargling, red spraying from her lips.

The man looked up from what he is doing, and saw me. "Come here, my angel," he said sweetly.

    "Come to your daddy."

His hand motioned for me to come to him, as he slowly lifted himself off my mother. As he stepped towards me, she lunged at his legs, clinging onto him. He pulled a handgun from his coat, looked at her, and pointed it at her face. "I told you, bitch, they're my kids too. You ain't ever leaving me." He said. "I'll see you in hell."

I heard a bang, and felt a warm spray hit my face and hair. He looked at me. I turned and ran as fast as I could, out the open front door. I could hear him screaming my name behind me. "Anny, you get back here now! Anny, don't make me mad, little girl! ANNY!" I heard him fall down the front steps, but I didn't turn to look back. I was alone in the dark, running, becoming one with the darkness. The ground, wet and cold from the storm that had passed through the evening, burning and cutting into my bare feet. Running through a treed area, I remembered the branches cutting my arms and face as I barreled through them.

Sunrise and I had found a swing set in some backyard. A tall fence around the yard at my back gave me a sense of security. Then I remember the boy. The boy, whose backyard I must have been in; the tall lanky boy, with glasses, and big brown eyes. The quiet boy who came to me, put a blanket around my shivering body, and wiped the blood off the side of my face, tucked a sticky piece of hair behind my ear. The boy, who sat on the cold ground in front of me in silence, held my hand, while we were waiting. The boy, who never broke eye-contact, even when the police officer was picking me up off the swing into his arms to carry me away. The boy who gave me a safe harbour in his eyes, that boy was LIAM.

Chapter Eleven

I had finally calmed down enough to get up off the floor. Hurried, and in a state of rage, I headed to the kitchen of the guest house. The slamming of the doors of the alcohol-free cupboards must have woken up Cassy.

"What the fuck is going on Anny? It's fucking two-thirty in the morning. We have to work at six am." She yelled at me.

"Nothing, fuck! Never mind! Where the hell is that bottle of rum? I know I saw it here the other day. WHERE IS IT? Instead of just standing there, help me find the fucking thing would ya?" I shrilled back at her.

She walked to the freezer, pulled out the bottle, and passed it to me gently. "Anny, what happened? What are you doing? Are you okay?" she asked in a low, concerned voice. "I'm sorry Cassy," I said, almost whispering, tears burning in my eyes. "I just can't right now. I'm sorry for yelling at you."

I slid down the cupboards to the floor, trying to hold back the tears that were now making their way down my cheeks. I opened the bottle and took a long hard swig. The rum was so cold it numbed my throat. I looked up at Cassy, who was looking down at me in shock. I gathered myself and wiped the tears from my face.

"Can you tell them I'm sick today, honey? Can you do that for me please?" I asked her, as I extend my hand up to her for help off the floor.

"Of course. Yeah, no problem," she answered me, pulling me up and into a hug. "You gonna be okay?" she asks.

"Yeah. I just need some air. I'm gonna get the fuck out of here for a bit, okay? Go back to bed. I'm sorry I woke you. We'll talk later today," I say.

I let her go and quickly found my shoes. Heading to the door, I didn't look back. I couldn't handle seeing Cassy or anyone right now. I couldn't answer questions I didn't even know the answers to. So I took my rage, and my bottle of rum, and headed out the door into the darkness.

My feet had a mind of their own, my mind so full of questions that it could not navigate them. I walked for what seemed for miles, only to come to my knees on a quiet, sandy beach. The moon was full and large. The storm must have passed quickly. I looked around the area that was lit up from the moon's glow. Taking in my surroundings, I recognised the cove. Cassy and I had passed by this place on one of our trips to the local market. Funny, we had not stopped to take in the beauty of it yet. At least I had it, the beauty and the sound of the waves rolling in. It was soothing, and I started to calm. As the waves rolled in crashing on the beach, so did my thoughts.

I was adopted by my fathers' sister, Maddilynn. How could that be? If my father was the man I just saw, how could the province allow that? How could I have never known any of this, if it were true? I knew that I had lived on the outskirts of town with my real parents. Sandy Bay, where I lived with Maddilynn, was only a short drive away. If this had happened, would it not have made national news? A family massacre, my father a member of the largest organized motorcycle club in the country, surely it would have been all over the papers and TV.

There were such large gaps in my memory from that time in my life. I would have to research this to find my answers. *What about Liam? How could that be? I moved and we went to the same school in Sandy Bay. How could it be that we lived so close prior to that? If it were true, why wouldn't he have told me? What about Peter? Did he know all of this? Being a member of the same club for as long as he had been, wouldn't he know their dirty little secrets?* I would have to wait and see what I could find out before talking to anyone about this. I resigned myself to that, and sat in the quiet beauty. I would wait until after sunrise to ensure that Cassy had left for the day, before heading back to try the WiFi and scan the internet for answers. The sunrise seemed to hold more colours than any I had ever seen before. An honesty of nature: real and naked, for all to see. My eyes were puffy from all the crying and I felt like I had been hit by a speeding bus. My legs, a little wobbly from the rum, stretched me up to standing position. I wiped off the sand from my backside, and headed for the guesthouse for some answers.

I tiptoed into the house, in case Cassy had decided to call in sick as well. Upon inspection of her room, I found that it was not the case. Thank God. I grabbed my laptop and searched for the WiFi password the hosts had written down.

There it was on the coffee table, with a note I had over-looked from Cassy saying:

Have a good day. Try and get some sleep.
I got your back where work is concerned
but you sooooo owe me an explanation when I get home!!

I connected to the WiFi, and found that they had not been lying when the said it would not be high speed. It was like nails on chalkboard waiting for the pages to load. After a couple of hours, there it was a front page article from August of 1982. **Massacre in Cripple Falls.** *It was real!* Scanning through the article, my heart stopped.

"A horrific scene was found this morning. The OPP were called to a local home in the small town of Cripple Falls. Constable Fred Woods of the Sandy Bay OPP detachment has stated that the cause of the deaths is not being released pending further investigation.

What could be commented on was that a man entered the home in the early hours of the morning, and had been responsible for taking the lives of both of his children, his wife, and himself. The man in question was identified as Bradley Omous, a known affiliate to the notorious Devil's Cradle motorcycle club. The police are giving no information with regards to any connection to the organization at this time

Constable Fred Woods! Oh my God Liam's last name was Woods. Was this his dad? The man killed both children! What? Why would they say that? Obviously I wasn't dead. I plugged my laptop into the complimentary house printer and made a copy. I kept on searching, and by the time I heard the screen door open, the floor was full of papers. Articles from different news papers, adoption regulations from the 1980s, any information I could find to help piece together the puzzle. I was so absorbed with the task, that by the time I looked up to see Cassy, she already had one of the papers in her hand, and had started reading.

"Anny, what is all of this?" She asked with both horror and curiosity.

"My life, I mean the missing bit." I answered, having a hard time looking her in the eyes.

"Come on. Step away from this for a while. There's a fresh bottle of shiraz with our name on it, screaming to be drunk on the deck." She said motherly.

And with that, I pulled myself away from the dirty splatter of my past all over the living room floor, and headed to the deck, for an evening of questions and answers.

Chapter Twelve

*I*t wasn't until China, that I could muster the courage to call Maddilynn. Cassy had questioned whether it was wise to continue on our journey, or to pack it in and head home. I had insisted that we continue. The last place I wanted to be was back in the midst of it all. I had too much anger in me to even approach the subject. Cassy very rarely strayed upon the subject anymore. I had told her what she needed to know, and she seemed satisfied with that.

We had spent the month of August in Thailand, in the north-most province of Chiang Rai. There was an abundance of volunteers in the small mountainous village. We were teaching English, and the pupils did not just extend to the children. The adults, from surrounding villages and the mountainous tribes' people, would often be amongst our classes. The location and the work was a welcome distraction from my mind. I had pushed everything into a dark corner, not willing to deal with it all yet. We slept in small buildings made of wood and soil. There was plenty of patching of roofs to be done, due to the constant pounding of the rainy season. We had bucket showers, and the bathroom facilities were primitive. The quiet nights, and busy days, somehow were helping.

Two weeks in Cambodia, in the city of Phnom Penh, was a relief from the heat of Thailand. The temperature was an average of twenty-two degrees. I had been working with disabled children at a local orphanage. HIV was rampant, and the disabled were rejected by their families and communities. It felt good to let some love into my heart. It was a slow pace in comparison to the previous teaching placements. The children I watched over were much quieter than the classrooms I was used to. Cassy had been working teaching in a different part of the city. In the evenings we would spend our time avoiding the subject of home, and eating sweet fruits and sticky rice.

The humidity in Hanoi Vietnam was unbearable, an average of eighty-five percent every day. This time we had a volunteer apartment, on the thirteenth floor of a high-rise apartment building. The breeze was helpful, especially after walking the stairs, when the elevator was out. We aided teachers at a local community centre. The days were long, and in the evenings it was so hot I barely slept. Every night, my mind turned to Liam and the events that had occurred in Bali.

Every night, there etched in my brain were those big brown eyes behind those little glasses, staring up at me. Every night I did the same thing, promised not to think about it anymore, and put it away, out of reach.

We had opted for a two month stretch in China. This would be the last of the volunteering for us. The next stop would be a paid stop, to line our pockets with cash for our return home. Xi'an was cold and dry. A strange change of pace it was to be wearing closed toe shoes and jackets. In December it started to dip down to near nine degrees. This time, Cassy and I both were working with children with disabilities. As Christmas was closing in, and we were nearing the end of our time there, I could feel that this job was going to be hard to leave. The extension of the placement there had made for some strong bonds.

I was amazed at the decorations for Christmas. Even though most of the people in the city were not Christian, it seemed that nearly every place I passed by had been decorated in some way. Home made paper lanterns hung from windows. Inside you could see trees lit up and decorated with paper chain-link garland. The children were excited as well. On the last day of class before holiday we even had Dun Che Lao, (old man Christmas), visit. Everyone was preparing for the Chinese New Year as well. Bowls of tangerines and oranges, displayed at local restaurants, symbolized wealth and good fortune. Pictures lined the halls of the apartment building we were staying at, of past relatives of residents, to honour them. The strange mesh of traditions was enriching. It all brought back thoughts of home and Christmas. Maddilynn had always tried to keep tradition in our small family. It was always dinner with her on Christmas day. I felt a twinge in my heart of both of love and betrayal.

Christmas day, Cassy and I decided that all we needed was liquor and music to mend our home sickness. Cassy had passed out, the lightweight she was, it was only mid-afternoon. Left up alone and full of liquid courage, I made the bad decision that I would call Maddilynn for a little Christmas greeting, and to finally confront her. I staggered to the local corner vender, and purchased an international calling card. The lobby of our apartment building had a pay phone, and I was grateful for that. I made my way to the phone, and after three unsuccessful number entries, the phone started to ring.

"Hello." I heard a raspy voice on the other end.

Fuck, I woke her up. The liquor had made me completely forget about the time difference. *It had to be two or three in the morning there.*

"MERRY FUCKING HO HO!" I slurred, half yelling from my end of the line.

"Anny? Anny, is that you? Where are you? Are you drunk?" I hear her say, sounding more alert.

"I'm in motherfucking China," I say laughing, and then changing my tone to pure evil, I spill out.

"And you will never guess what Santa brought me this year: My memory is back. Guess what I have? A fucking file folder full of articles about how my dad slaughtered my family. Oh yeah! Funny, though, how it doesn't mention that hey, I'm not fucking dead, or hey, that he shot my mother in her fucking face, right fucking in front of me. That's right, right before he tried to kill me. Awesome! So I have some questions for you, like how the hell could you keep this from me?"

"Annabella Moreen Omous, I don't care where you are, or how drunk you are. You back off of that tone with me girl, or I will fly to where you are and kick your ass!" She spat.
I straightend my posture instantly, and remembered who I am talking to. The one thing Maddilynn did not allow was disrespect. There was a sigh from the end of the phone.

"Baby girl, I am so sorry that this is happening, that any of this happened. You not remembering, it was a gift from God. When your other memories of childhood started to fade in your teens, I thought that maybe it was a side effect of the initial blackout. You never seemed to let it bug you, and I was not going to bring that pain back into your life." Maddilynn's tone had quieted.

"How did they even let me come and stay with you? You were living so close to where it happened. I mean you were his family?" I asked.

"That's exactly why, because I am your family. His actions were not mine. I distanced myself from any mutual associates, and pushed for you to come and stay with me. They kept the news going that you were dead to keep any issues from the club arising, with regards to you and your safety. When they realized that you blacked out what happened, they allowed you to come and stay with me. They had conditions, though. I could have absolutely nothing to do with the club, or any of your Uncles in the club. They enforced it too. The cop, umm .. Woods, the one whose backyard they found you in. He took a special interest in you. He was a real pain in my ass. He moved two blocks away from us, and would check in unexpectedly all the time. He would bring his kid... Liam. You guys would play all the time. Peas in a pod, we would call you. It was only when you moved out he stopped checking in," she explained.

Oh my God. It was all coming together now.

"What happened? Why did he do it? I don't understand," I asked her.

"Your mom, she had enough of his drinking, and fucking around. He hit her one too many times. She started talking to the cops. She wanted out, and she was going to take you guys with her. She didn't want you two growing up and ending up in the life. She was trying to protect you. He found out. The reach of the club is far, and somehow he found out. He got piss drunk, rode to the house, and snapped. That's what I know," she said.

"And look at the life I chose!" I said, defeated.

"I tried baby, I did, to keep you from them. It wasn't long after that your Uncles found out you were alive. They stayed away because they had to, but as soon as you were old enough they came looking for you. Your dad made them promise to look out for you. It was their way of protecting you is all." She got quiet for a minute and then said, "You okay with all of this?"

"No, yes, I don't know. But thank you, mom. I needed to know." I replied. I rarely called her mom.

I could hear the lump in her throat as she said "Take care of your-self, Merry Christmas, my love. Bye."

"Merry Christmas, I love you too. Bye." I said, hanging up the phone.

I finally had some answers. The puzzle was solved. I was not happier for knowing, just satisfied in having some clarity. *But what about Liam? He knew this whole time, and not a little bit, all of it. We hung out! Peas in a pod! What the hell!* I was pissed. I took a swig of my traveler mug of rum and coke, and decided on the second bad decision of the day. I didn't care what time it was, or where he was. I needed to give him a piece of my mind. *Apparently we were best of friends, so fuck it,* I thought. *I'm entitled to spread the joy of this situation.* The phone started ringing, two rings, and three rings. *Oh good,* I was losing my nerve as it rung. I hadn't talked to him since the blow out in the parking lot. I was just getting comfortable to leave a voice mail, when on the fourth ring; "Hello Inspector Woods speaking." He said. *Oh fuck, I forgot he's a cop. He has to answer his cell. Shit.* My inner voice reminds me. I stayed silent on the other end of the phone.

"Hello, I can hear you. Is everything okay?" He said, sounding so professional.

"I know everything Liam." I say in a slow low tone. "I know everything, and I cannot believe you kept this from me."

"Anny?" He stumbled for a moment.

"Yes Anny! How could you? We hung out all the time. Like what the fuck, you were there?" I was starting to speed through my words. Emotions were bubbling up, a mix of anger, sadness and missing him all at once.

"Anny I... I," he tried to get a word in edgewise.

"No! No you don't get to talk now!" I yell at him. In the background I hear a women's voice asking who it is. "You knew how I felt for you. What was it, some sort of ploy to find shit out for your job? Was I work for you? Was I? This was not some crush or fling for me. I know that now. How could it be? I have loved you since before I knew you. But don't worry, you didn't break my heart," I started to say, unable to control my tears, I start to weep. "You shattered it. You fucking shattered it!" And with that, I slammed down the phone.

Chapter Thirteen

*T*he five months, and three weeks, we had been in Tokyo had flown by. The city was a buzz of activity, so many people, so much to do. We had been making some decent money, nothing too crazy, but enough to get by. If we budgeted right, we would each go home with about ten grand in our pockets.

We had been hired by an agency to teach English to higher-up corporate businessmen, whose travels abroad demanded it. The job was easy. Both Cassy and I were having a blast.

We had set up camp at a hostel called the Oak Hotel. It was decently priced at around seven hundred and fifty dollars Canadian each a month. The place was clean, and the rooms were quite larger than we had thought they would be. Each room had a single bed, TV, desk, WiFi, refrigerator, and our own private bathroom. We had been making so many friends of other travelers coming in and out of the hostel; our journals barely had any room left for more contact information to be recorded in them.

The hotel was located in the most historic area in Tokyo, between Veno and the traditional area called Asakusa. There was a Seven Eleven on the corner, and a Star Bucks at the end of the block. How we had missed good coffee. Our favourite place to eat was at Johnathan's Restaurant. It was kind of a divey looking place, but the owners were always cheerful towards us, and their prices were really reasonable. A meal was only one thousand yen, (about ten dollars Canadian), which was cheap. One thing about Japan, it was easy to go through money.

Some evenings we would go to Roppongi, the night club district, and party. We had made some resident friends through work that were a bit younger. Still, I had no problem keeping up. Cassy on the other hand, (being the light weight that she was), was always ready to leave first. I was glad she was so tiny, considering how many times I basically had to carry her home.

We had been to Veno Park, and seen the national museum, and the zoo. We stared in awe at the Sensoji Temple. We had looked over the city from the Tokyo tower. We even got a trip into the famous Tsukiji fish market, where Cassy kept trying to get me to eat octopus. All in all, it had been the perfect way to end the adventure.

I could tell Cassy was ready to go home. She and her husband Chris had been skyping every night. We had made appointments at a local salon, the day before our flight, to get some beauty treatments, so we would look hot when we got back. My hair was a wreck. I decided I would change it from the red I had grown so fond of, to a black with electric blue tips. How better to leave Japan, than with a cool Japanese alternative hair cut. The look was hot in Tokyo. I had her cut it wispy on the one side, angling it towards my chin. God I had lost weight. My face could certainly handle a shorter cut now. I loved it. The blue even matched some of the new flowers I had added to my back tattoo representing the new places I had seen. I was going back a whole new person, unrecognizable to even myself, and I liked that.

After our pampering, we treated ourselves to a nice meal at a more expensive restaurant. Cassy was ecstatic to get home. She was giggling every few minutes. It was contagious, especially after a few drinks of shochu. Both of us laughing at nothing caused a few dirty looks. When I tried to apologize to the neighbouring patrons, I mixed up my words and said basically, sorry for licking you, instead of sorry for disturbing you. Cassy, mid drink, she laughed so hard she spit her drink so far it hit the next table. We both burst out laughing, and called for the bill.

Our flight from Naritia International Airport was at five pm the next day. We needed to get there four hours early for some reason. With all we had to do in the next twenty-four hours, Cassy and I said our good nights and retired to our rooms. I had already packed everything, and was ready for the trip. I pulled out my laptop. I had been working on some videos for friends, with picture compilations, and clever messages. Going through some more pictures, I decided I would be brave, and do what I had been dreading, update my status on Facebook. I hadn't been on in over a year. I was only dreading seeing the happy couple, Amber and Liam, spread across my computer screen, clawing at me like some feral cat. They were to have had a June wedding. Being that it was now the end of June, it should still be pretty fresh news. I hadn't spoken with Liam since China, nor did I have any intention of it. In-fact, I decided to myself I could easily solve the problem and simply un-friend him.

Logging in, my stomach started to turn into knots. As I watched the screen pop up, I held my breath. I breathed out. *Nothing, hum, that's weird.* I thought. Then I had a sinking feeling. *Oh of course he un-friended me. Why wouldn't he, after my crying screaming fit on the phone. Who cares? You were going to un-friend him anyway.* I say to myself. I scrolled down the news feed, as rest of the page was still loading. Nothing, not a blip, a like, or shared anything. I notice the chat turn on, on the side of the screen, and then I looked up. *Holy shit two hundred and twenty-five messages.*

I clicked on my messages, and my heart started to pound. Amongst the few random notes from other friends, Liam had sent two hundred and sixteen messages. I closed the lid of the laptop and pushed it away, as if it were going to attack me. I walked away from the desk, pacing trying to think.

This was supposed to be done. My inner voice was on fire. *This was supposed to be done.*

I had already resigned myself to that fact. It was compounded by everything that had happened, and his words of reasoning to me that day in the parking lot. I had already spoken to Peter. I was heading home. We would try a second round, crazy or not. My life belonged with the club. I had a job lined up to start in August. My ducks were in a row. *Just delete the messages Anny. Be done with this!* My inner voice was screaming at me, but I couldn't. As usual, when it came to Liam, I had no control over myself. Lifting the screen, I started to read his messages. So many of them:

Anny I'm sorry. You don't understand. You have it all wrong. I never used you. I have feelings for you too. Anny I'm sorry. Where are you? Why won't you talk to me? Call me." Over, and over, there were similar messages with apologies, confessions of his feelings, and assurances of his intentions.

But the one message that stood out, the one I read over a hundred times, read;

"Anny, I didn't marry Amber. I couldn't, not now. Please call me when you get this. I love you. I always have.

Chapter Fourteen

*T*he entry through Canada customs had been a daunting task. Vancouver airport was busy. The early summer traffic of large Canadian tourists, and parents looking exhausted, dragging their screaming children through the umpteenth line up, was enough to make you want to scream. The air conditioning must have been acting up. I could feel the sweat on my brow. Not a good look when you are about to be scrutinized by some pissed off, underpaid, border control officer.

As I passed my passport to the large growly man, I already knew I was going to be searched. Cassy was just being handed her passport back at the second desk down from me, when I heard the officer say, "Open your bag please, Ma'am."

I could see Cassy looking curiously at me, a little impatient.

"Hold on girl. Tattoos and an alternative hair style, equals SEARCH," I yelled over to her. The officer shot a dirty look my way. I countered with a well isn't it true shrug back.

He kind of half-grinned, and then said, "Thank you for your patience Ma'am. Welcome back to Canada."

"For sure," I half-huffed under my breath, as I grabbed my panties out of his hand, and shoved them back into my bag full of other violated personal items.

"Welcome to Canada!" I said, as I approached Cassy. She shook her head and laughed a little.

"We should check the status of our next flight!" She said excitedly. You could see the excitement dripping from her. It had been a great trip, but a year away from the husband is a long time, way too long for Cassy. I looked at her from the corner of my eye in wonderment. I only wished I'd felt an inkling of the same excitement, but all I could feel was dread. Dread of the homecoming I was avoiding the last year. Dread of the truth of what I felt. Dread of going back to the same life I had just travelled half way around the world to escape.

"There it is on the board there Air Canada to Toronto on time - three o'clock."

"Three o'clock," she said. "Well I guess we have a couple of hours to kill. I'm gonna give Chris a call, and let him know we've made it back to Canada." She hustled off towards the bank of pay phones.

I glanced up at the board, trying to shake off the negative feelings.

Great. On time, it couldn't be delayed EH? Any other fucking time, but no not today! My inner voice muttered on.

As I stared at the board, trying to will it to change, my breath left my body. A sense of panic that you feel right before you get into a sparring match hit me. That flight or flight response reserved for the moments that leave you feeling most alive. For right directly underneath the listing for the flight to Toronto read:

Air Canada   Winnipeg   4:30   ON TIME

"You gonna call Peter?" I barely hear her say, my eyes still glued to the board, body still vacant of breath.

"ANNY YOU GONNA CALL PETER?" She repeated herself, and gave me a nudge.

"Um what, um no." I could feel my face turning red, stumbling on my words I reply, "I'll call him when we land. He'll be busy now any way." I peddled around the subject. *There that should hold off anymore questioning about it.*

We headed to the food court for a snack. While scarfing down on our twelve dollar, made fresh yesterday, sandwiches, my mind was in a fog. I was dumbstruck with feeling. I knew what I wanted to do. *But that was fucking crazy right? No, you have to go home. Your life is there. Everything you need is there. Was it?* I already knew the answer to that. *If it was, I wouldn't be feeling this now.*

"Darling, were the fuck are you right now?" I hear Cassy snap at me. I had been half paying attention to her, going on about something about the new bathroom Chris had put in while we were abroad, but I couldn't muster the energy to give a fuck about whether she should paint it green or blue.

"Blue." I answered back. "Sorry I'm a bit jet lagged is all, defiantly blue."

There, I had given her an answer. Hopefully it would be the right one. My mind was elsewhere, spinning and racing into places it should not be heading.

An hour and half later, sitting in the boarding area, I was still captured by my own thoughts. Cassy had found her laptop and was updating her Facebook status to ARRIVED. *Thank God for free WiFi,* was all I could think. She was keeping herself busy, and allowing me to sit in quiet. I kept staring at the screen on the wall, *Winnipeg, four-thirty.* My body felt like pins and needles. My heart was speeding up, *Winnipeg, four-thirty.*

"AIR CANADA FLIGHT A1725 TO TORONTO NOW BOARDING. PASSANGERS FROM SEATS A1 TO B22 PLEASE HEAD TO THE BOARDING PLATFORM." The loud speaker shot me from my thoughts.

FUCK, why did we splurge on the good seats? I wasn't ready to board!

"YEAHH, THAT'S US! COME ON!" Cassy squealed.

She grabbed my arm, and was dragging me behind her, toward the perky air hostess at the desk. My legs felt like stone. Every step took every ounce of my strength to muster.

My peripheral vision was on overdrive. I was having an out of body experience, so surreal. Watching Cassy hand her ticket to the lady was in slow motion. Now it was my turn. I see her hand gesture to me. I, still holding the ticket, hand it to her, and in that brief second I lost my mind.

The hostess looks at me queer, as I am still clenching the ticket.

"Miss, will you be flying with us today?" she asked, as she tried to pry the ticket from my grip."Miss?"

I ripped the ticket from her hand, and reply, "No not today, thank you." I could see the look of shock and bewilderment crossing Cassy's face. Then almost in a split of a second, you could see her mind piecing together the puzzle.

"Those pictures weren't for Peter were they?" she said over the air hostess's shoulder.

I gave her a shake of my head in answer.

She smiled and said, "Be careful, girl. They're the ones that break your heart!"

She turned, waved her hand in the air, and shouted, "Call me, crazy one! Love ya!"

As I watched her walk away, I knew she was right. I was fucking crazy. I ran to the line for tickets. My head pounding and heart racing, I was dying waiting in line. Finally I was next.

"Next." I heard the portly airport employee shout.

I made my way to the counter. "I would like to cash in this ticket to Toronto, and purchase one to Winnipeg please." I said with determination. As the lady started the process, my mind started to drift again.

"Is that one way to Winnipeg or return?" The woman asked. I stared blankly at her for a second, contemplating my next action.

"One way, or return? Ma'am?" She asked again.

I stared her directly in the eye, as if to challenge her, and replied, "One way."

Chapter Fifteen

*S*unset, on an. other wise uneventful, Wednesday evening, and Liam was relaxing after a long day at work. A knock at the door caught his attention. He lifted his long, lean body from the couch. Reaching for a t-shirt, he headed towards the door.

He pulled the shirt on, covering his well-defined abs, and opened the door.

"Are you Liam, sir?" A middle aged East Indian man asked him.

"Ah yes, who are you?" Liam asked, puzzled.

The man handed him a bag and said, "Delivery for you, sir."

"From whom?" Liam questioned the man with a stern voice.

"I do not know, sir. I am just doing my job, what I am told to do. Good evening Sir," the man replied. He turned and headed off the porch towards the driveway. Liam, bewildered, wandered onto the porch to watch the man get into his cab and drive away. He headed into the house, closing the door behind him. His curiosity was peeked. *What the hell was that?* He thought to himself. He placed the bag on the kitchen counter and investigated its contents. Inside, he found a six-pack of beer, and a DVDR with a sticky note attached to it. The note read:

You said that beer makes you brave.

I need you brave right now.

Open one and play the DVDR.

Anny.

Completely puzzled, he proceeded to do as he was told. He loaded the DVDR, cracked a beer, and sat down on the couch. He turned on the TV, a little anxious to see what this could be. The DVDR began to play. Pictures of Anny from around the world, holding signs in a message form to him. The sweet sound of the Kye Kye's song "Trees and Trust" was the background to the project. She was standing in the same spot in each frame, while the background sped by behind her. All of the pictures were beautiful, but it was the last frame, and the last message, that made his heart jump for a second. The video message read;

HI

I HAVE TRAVELLED

HALF THE WORLD

AND SEEN

THE MOST AMAZING
BEAUTIFUL THINGS
BUT NO
BEAUTY CAN
COMPARE TO
THE BEAUTY OF
WHAT I FEEL
FOR YOU
I HAVE TRIED
TO FORGET YOU
BUT I CAN'T
I HAVE THOUGHT
OF YOU EVERY DAY
SO I HAVE
TRAVELLED
9,863 KMS
TO ASK YOU
IF YOU THINK
YOU CAN
GIVE THIS

A CHANCE
NOW I NEED
SOME BRAVERY
SO CAN U BRING ME
A BEER 2

The last frame of the video was still on the screen staring at him. A picture of Anny, holding that sign in front of his house. As he stepped onto the porch he saw her standing in the driveway. He leaned his arms on the railing, and shook his head.

"You're fucking crazy, you know?" he said, and then smiled.

She looked up at him coyly; a sweet grin on her lips, and said. "Yeah, but I think you kinda like it."

He cracked the beer in his hand, extended it out to her, and said, "Yeah, I think I do too."

THE GUILD

Anny Omous

Chapter Two

*T*he cabin was one of the many safe houses owned by the club. Nestled in the Almeguin Highlands a mere two and a half hour drive from the city, it was a perfect refuge from any watchful eyes. It sat on a two hundred acre parcel of land and had only seasonal road access. The title to the land was listed to a strip club owner in the city with whom the Devil's Cradle had become silent partners. The cabin was only used for club business and by titled members only. The land had a few outbuildings, a pond and plenty of hardwood acres of bush.

The nearest neighbour was a ten-minute walk, and in an area made up of people in retirement or looking for privacy and escape from the city, it was a perfect place to conduct any business that needed the shield of silence.

The cabin itself was small in nature housing a single bedroom, and a one room living room-slash-kitchen area with a large stone fireplace. Designed in a simpler time, it had no electricity or running water, but did have a root cellar that was accessible by a panel in the floor in the kitchen. The cellar had no windows and a dirt floor. It smelt of must and mould. It had been transformed into a perfect holding cell for anyone the club thought needed a little encouragement and time to expel any information it deemed necessary, that someone may be withholding under the guise of morality.

Cassy sat in the dankness of the cellar unaware if it had been two days or three that she had been held captive. Her body ached from the punishment she had received from Peter when she was unable to answer his line of questioning regarding Anny and her whereabouts. Though she cursed Anny for her predicament she couldn't help to wonder why this friend she held so close had lived a life she never knew, and all at once she understood why Anny had fled. Her mind turned to her husband. God how she missed him. Certainly the police were looking for her by now. *Anytime they would be there to save her. Wouldn't they?* She kept that thought in her mind, picturing them there to take her home, the only place she wanted to be.

Her legs were numb from the coldness of the ground and though she feared what may be rustling in the darkness around her she feared it less than the next time she would be called for questioning, which most certainly would be soon. She tried to hold her tears of fear back and remain as silent as possible as she heard the footsteps above her and scraping of chairs being moved. She strained to make out what the muffled voices above her were saying, praying that they would forget her existence below them.

As she heard the creaking of the hatch opening, chills ran up her spine. She turned her head and leaned her body into the dampness of the rock wall foundation willing herself to disappear into it and become invisible. "Hello darling. It's time to talk again," she heard Peter say in a low tone. "Come on, up and at em."

She pulled herself up and tried to maintain her composure as Peter extended his hand towards her. He helped her as she weakly climbed the stairs into the light, so bright it blinded her. He escorted her to the table and chair that she had become accustomed to as her throne of despair.

Peter circled her slowly. Staring at her like prey. In his mind he had started to question if she was telling the truth about not knowing Anny's whereabouts, but he had come to a point of no turning back. He knew he had maybe one or more interrogations with her until she succumbed to her injuries or he would have to end this with or without answers. This was not a reality he wanted to accept.

"Cassy, I know that this last while we have spent together has not been comfortable for you. I know you miss your family and want to see them. I want that too. I'm not a man without family values. That's why this is happening. Anny needs to come home to her family. She needs to atone for her actions and explain why she would choose anything else but her family. I think even if you do not know where she is you can come up with a solution as to how we may figure that out. Do you have any ideas as to how sweetheart?" He said in a sweet tone.

"I don't know. I'm so tired. I don't know." Cassy whimpered. Peter grabbed her by the back of the neck and forced her head onto the table hard. He pulled a hunting knife from its sheath from his belt and garnered it to her face. Spit landed on her cheek as he shouted into her ear, "Well fucking think!"

He released her from his grip and grabbed her hand,

placing it on the table, holding it at her wrist. Tears started to run down her face as her mind raced trying to come up with a solution. She looked up at the three other men in the room and noticed one of them casually playing on his cell phone. Peter slowly pressed the knife hard into her pinky finger slicing the knife across it in a saw like motion, drawing blood. Cassy screamed out, "Wait I know! I know how to find her!"

Peter pulled the knife away and let her hand go. "How?" he asked her. "Facebook .... I can message her and ask. It may even show where she is."

She answered suddenly animated with a glimmer of hope of surviving the situation. "Do you have Facebook and messenger on your phone?" She posed the question to the young prospect who she had observed playing on his cell.
"Yeah!" he responded.
"Well fucking give her you phone!" Peter yelled at him.

Bashfully, he handed Cassy his cell. Peter stood behind

her as she logged herself in to Facebook. She checked to see if Anny was available for chat and let out a sigh, "She's on here. Let me message her and see if she will respond."

"Do it," Peter said, trying to appear calm.

Hey girl. What's up? Where are you?

Cassy messaged Anny.

Time seemed to stop as Cassy awaited a reply from Anny. She could hear her heart pounding and wondered if the others in the room could as well.

Finally she heard the popping sound of Anny typing a response.

Doing well. Can't talk right now but will call you soon. Sorry I had to bail like that. Hope you and Chris are having fun. Miss you! Luv ya! I will explain everything when I call.

Anny responded.

"How the fuck does that help?" Peter screamed at

Cassy.

"Look right here," Cassy pointed at the phone, "it says sent from Winnipeg Manitoba, right here."

Peter grabbed the phone from Cassy's hand and stared at it. All at once, he pieced it together, "Sneaky Fucking Bitch!!"

Peter's mind flashed back to a moment not too long before. A moment that had stuck with him and always bothered him. He rubbed his left hand as he recalled his time spent under interrogation with the large beast of a cop named Inspector Woods. The man he remembered that seemed to know Anny and her business better than just through surveillance. It had always bothered him that he had addressed her as Anny and not Annabella like any other cop that had mentioned her. It also had made him wonder how he had known about his and Annys' altercation on Christmas Eve when she had found him with the whore he was enjoying. Most of all it had always bothered him that the Inspector had seemed so enraged when he had told him that Anny was being a fucking bitch and deserved what she got, that he had felt it necessary to dislocate Peters' thumb and break his two of his fingers. It had taken two other officers to remove the man off of him. Peter was certain that it would have escalated if they had not arrived when they had. Now he knew. It all made sense. His rage was spewing out of him. The humiliation of her actions would not go unpunished. Their years together and everything they had been through only to be betrayed.

He whipped the phone against the wall, smashing it into pieces. "FUCKING WHORE! FUCK! FUCK! FUCK!!" He screamed smashing his fists off the table. "I'm gonna fucking kill her!" he shrilled before driving the hunting knife into the table, just missing Cassy's hand.

He turned his back to the others and faced the wall. His shoulders moved up and down like an animal trying to breathe out its rage. Cassy sank down into her chair avoiding eye contact with any of the men in the room, trying not to make a sound.

"Boss, what do we now? Do we let her go?" asked the large prospect.

Peter let out a long sigh and paused for the longest time. Still facing the wall, he responded, "Call Sonny. Get him here now. If he gives you any hell just tell him it's about Anny."

"Okay, I'm on it." He said and then exited the cabin to make the call.

"What about her, and my phone?" the young prospect asked. "Do I bring her home?"

"Fuck your phone dip shit!" Peter snarled and then turned around. "No I got a better idea."

He reefed the knife from the table, grabbed Cassy's hand and pinned it down. "You're gonna ensure she comes home, beautiful," he said as he pierced the knife into Cassy's pinky. Cassy looked at him in horror and screamed, "Oh my god! No! No! Please no!"

www.ingramcontent.com/pod-product-compliance
Lightning Source LLC
Chambersburg PA
CBHW052140170626
46812CB00004B/1521

* 9 7 8 0 9 9 3 8 9 3 3 4 6 *